Vachon

Wingman on Ice

by Matt Christopher

Illustrated by Karin Lidbeck

Little, Brown and Company

Boston   New York   Toronto   London

to
Brenda, Bruce, Barbara, Beverly and Bradley

Text copyright © 1964, 1993 by Matthew F. Christopher
Illustrations copyright © 1993 by Karin Lidbeck

First Paperback Edition

ISBN 0-316-14269-7
Library of Congress Catalog Card Number 64-16549

10 9 8 7 6 5 4 3 2 1

MV-NY

Published simultaneously in Canada
by Little, Brown & Company (Canada) Limited

Printed in the United States of America

Wingman on Ice

Bantam Hockey League
Roster of the White Knights

Buck Fillis   *Coach*

Line 1

1	*Jim Smith*	*goalie*
2	*Ed Jones*	*right forward*
3	*Larry Thomas*	*left forward*
4	*Joe Farmer*	*center*
5	*Al Burns*	*right defense*
6	*Duck Franks*	*left defense*
7	*Andy Marr*	*substitute*

Line 2

8	*Tim Collins*	*goalie*
9	*Tod Baker*	*right forward*
10	*Jim Wright*	*left forward*
11	*Skip Haddock*	*center*
12	*Biff Jones*	*right defense*
13	*Snowball Harry Carr*	*left defense*
14	*Bud Wooley*	*substitute*

Line 3

15	*Joe Easter*	*goalie*
16	*Tom Cash*	*right forward*
17	*Bert Stevens*	*left forward*
18	*Adam Wink*	*center*
19	*Mickey Share*	*right defense*
20	*Tony Nadali*	*left defense*
21	*Mark Malone*	*substitute*

1

A STICK SLAPPED the puck hard, and the flat, rubber disk shot across the ice like a black dot. It struck the boards, bounced off, and Tod Baker stopped it with the blade of his hockey stick.

He hardly looked up as he dug his right skate into the ice and pushed himself forward. With both hands on the stick he started to dribble the puck down the ice. He shifted the stick blade from one side of the puck to the other, easing it gently each time.

A player rushed at him from his left side. Quickly, Tod picked up speed.

Then it happened. He struck the puck harder than he should have, and it shot too far to his right. Desperately, he sped after it. But another skater hooked it with his stick and dribbled it away.

"Why didn't you pass it?" a voice snapped near his elbow.

Tod looked around and saw Skip Haddock glaring at him. Skip was center for the White Knights. He was tall and willowy and handled a hockey stick as if he had been born with one in his hand.

"I'm sorry," murmured Tod.

Another voice cut in sharply. "Quit talking there and let's get after that puck!"

It was Buck Fillis, the coach. He was on skates, a tall man wearing a hat and a heavy

4

blue and white sweater. A whistle dangled on a cord around his neck.

This was a scrimmage game among themselves. Next Saturday morning the White Knights were going to scrimmage the Trojans. The regular Bantam League games started the Saturday after that.

Coach Fillis had picked two squads, A and B, to play against each other this Saturday morning. The A squad wore white jerseys over their sweaters to distinguish them from the B's. Tod was on the A squad, playing right forward.

In the Bantam Hockey League, the teams were composed of three lines each. Each line had its own forwards, defensemen and goalie.

But today Coach Fillis did not group his team into lines. Some kids were a little older than others, so he had selected two squads to let the younger boys play on the same squads as the older ones. In this way the squads were evenly matched, and every player could practice and learn to play better hockey.

5

Tod was glad that Coach Fillis had his White Knights team work out that way. A younger player could learn a lot by playing along with an older player.

The B squad got the puck past the red line that crossed the middle of the ice. Snowball Harry Carr stole it and snapped it back. Another B player shot up behind him and stopped it with his skate. He kicked it forward, then slapped it with his stick.

Tod and Skip came charging up the ice together. For a moment the puck was free. A B squad player went after it. Skip gave him a body-check, and the player lost his balance and fell. Skip always did this when he had a chance. Tod thought that Skip just enjoyed body-checking, even if he didn't always do it legally.

Skip stopped dead, ice chips spraying from his skates. Another opponent was approaching fast. Skip passed the puck to Tod. Tod stopped it and looked around. An A player was down near the boards. Tod smacked the puck to him. The player caught it with the blade of his stick and started with it across the other team's blue line.

Tod sped down center ice. It was clear sailing ahead. If he got the puck he might be able to smack it past the goalie.

"Here! Pass it here!" he shouted.

The puck skittered across the ice toward him. It was a good pass. He tried to stop it with the heel of his stick. But the puck struck the stick and glanced off. Disgustedly, Tod turned and went after it, his skates cutting short, curved grooves in the ice.

Skip Haddock reached the puck first. He dribbled it at an angle in front of the goal. Tod could see the goalie crouched in front of the net, trying to keep himself between it and Skip.

Then, just as Skip glided past the net, he snapped the puck. Like a bullet it shot between the goalie and the side of the net.

Score!

Buck Fillis blew the whistle. "Nice shot, Skip!" he said as he came skating down the ice. "But, you, Tod — you should have stopped that puck and gone for the goal yourself. You're not holding that blade flat on the ice. Bend it in a little toward the puck when trying to stop it, and then ease it away from the puck when they meet. That small rubber beast can get away from you in a hurry if you don't treat it just right."

Tod nodded.

"You're not stickhandling right, either," the coach went on. "You're not supposed to hit the puck — just push it. Treat it as if it were a raw egg."

Snowball Harry Carr laughed. "Good thing it isn't, Coach," he said. "This rink would be a mess!"

The boys laughed. Even Tod had to grin.

Buck had substitutes come in for both squads. Skip, Tod and Snowball were among those he sent out for a rest. They breathed hard as they sat on the players' bench behind the boards.

Tod didn't really feel tired, though. He wished he could stay in there. The ice here on Manna Rink was smooth as glass. There weren't cracks or bumps on it like there were on the ice pond in the field near home.

The rink was just beautiful. That red line through the middle, those blue lines about twenty feet away on either side of it, the wide circle in the center and those four big circles in the end zones for face-offs — you really felt like playing hockey here.

Wish I had a new stick, thought Tod as he looked sadly at the one in his gloved hands. It was probably older than he. Coach Fillis had given it to him. The coach had probably used it himself years ago, although he had not said so. Anyway, it sure looked bruised and battered.

Christmas is only three days away. Maybe Mom and Dad will get a hockey stick for me.

That's what I want most of all. A new hockey stick.

Tod and the other boys sitting on the bench watched Buck Fillis drop the puck for the face-off as the scrimmage continued. In less than a minute the B squad scored a goal, and a few moments later the A squad evened it up. After three minutes, Coach Fillis changed players again making sure that every member of his White Knights team had equal time on the ice.

At last he called the scrimmage off, because another team was waiting to play.

In the locker room Coach Fillis urged the boys to skate as much as possible wherever they could find ice to skate on. "Skate backwards all you can," he said. "Make quick turns. Quick stops and starts. Get a puck if you don't have one and practice passing. And dribbling." He looked at Tod, his eyes twinkling. "Remember, Tod, treat that puck as if it were a raw egg."

The locker room echoed with laughter from all twenty-one boys.

10

Buck Fillis was a great coach. A real friendly guy.

The boys took off their skates and put on their shoes. Some of them covered the blades of their skates with a rubber protector and walked out with their skates on. Tod had no protector for his skates.

He rode home with Biff Jones and Biff's father in their car.

Three days till Christmas, he thought anxiously. *Just three days.*

2

RIGHT AFTER BREAKFAST Sunday morning Tod changed into his skating clothes. He put on a windbreaker, his winter hat, mittens and boots and walked to the ice pond in Mr. Terriwell's field.

He ploughed through the path that had already been made through the foot-deep snow that covered the ground. A strong wind whipped up powdery snow against his face. The sun was a golden disk in the almost cloudless sky. It made the snow sparkle. And it made him squint.

He had wanted Jane to go along with him. She didn't want to. She preferred to look at the funnies in today's paper. Well, he enjoyed the funnies, too. But he'd look at them later.

He soon reached the top of the knoll and could see the ice pond. He had hoped no one would be there and no one was. He wanted the whole ice pond for himself so that he could practice dribbling and stickhandling and not worry about someone laughing at him.

He reached the pond, sat on the bench that Mr. Terriwell himself had put there, and changed his boots for his skates. They were regular hockey skates, with arch supports in the shoes and hard toe caps. This was the second winter that he had used them.

Laces tied tightly, he rose from the bench and

13

stepped onto the ice. The snow on it looked as if it had been sprinkled on with a giant saltshaker.

He skated all around the pond for a while, then did the figure eight frontwards and backwards. After about five minutes he dropped the puck on the ice and concentrated on dribbling.

Move the puck with smooth, side-to-side sweeps with the blade of the stick, Coach Fillis had told the boys. And that's what Tod did. But when he skated faster he either went by the puck or hit it too hard.

Tod clamped his teeth on his lower lip as he tried and tried to become master of that puck. At last he became so angry he struck the puck hard and sent it sailing over the ice. It pierced the bank of snow and lay buried so deep inside of it that Tod couldn't find it for a long while. When he did, he was angry at himself for losing his temper. He quit and started for home. Jane would be coming after him for lunch soon, anyway.

14

After lunch, Jane and Tod both went to the ice pond. Tod took his puck and hockey stick with him again.

Jane was in the third grade. She had long black hair full of curls, but that was because Mom fixed them that way. Otherwise, they would be straight as strings, and Jane didn't want her hair straight as strings.

Marylou Farmer, who was in Jane's grade, and her brother Joe were already at the pond. So was Jack Evans, a tall, dark-haired boy who had been on the same team with Tod last year. Tod liked him a lot. He was sorry that Jack was on another team. But it wasn't Jack's choice. At the start of each season the coaches picked their teams. No two years were the teams the same.

They greeted Tod and Jane.

"Been hoping you'd bring your puck," said Jack. "I brought my stick along, too. So did Joe."

Tod let the boys play with the puck while he put on his skates. Then he, Joe and Jack passed

15

the puck among themselves. Joe was good. The coach had said he'd have Joe play center on Line 1, which meant that he wouldn't be playing with Tod. Tod was on Line 2, and Line 2's center was Skip Haddock.

More people showed up at the pond — boys, girls and grown-ups, too. Among them were Skip Haddock and Tim Collins. Tim was goalie on Line 2. He was a husky, dark-haired boy who never talked much. You wouldn't think he'd be the kind of guy Skip would pal around with, but Skip did.

The boys took over one end of the ice pond in a game of shinny. Skip, Tim and Joe passed the puck among themselves as if the puck and their hockey sticks were natural cousins. Tod felt as if he didn't belong with them. He could skate fast frontwards and backwards and turn quickly — almost better than any one of them — but he was far from being a good stickhandler. The puck and his stick were just plain enemies.

It's the hockey stick, that's what it is, Tod told himself. *The toe and heel are worn so badly that the blade doesn't meet the puck as it should. Boy, I hope I get a new stick for Christmas!*

Tim passed the puck to Tod again. It struck his blade and glanced off as it usually did. This time Tod raced after it hard. He dug his skates into the ice and pumped his legs as fast as if he were competing in a one-hundred-yard sprint. The puck slid out of their skating area and skimmed over the ice among the other skaters.

Just as Tod reached the puck and was about to stop it with his stick, a small boy got in front of him. Tod struck him solidly, and the boy went sprawling on the ice.

Fright gripped Tod as he skated swiftly over to him.

"Jimmie!" he cried as he recognized five-year-old Jimmie Lamarr. "I'm sorry! Are you all right?"

17

Jimmie's face was screwed up in pain. "I —
I'm all right," he said.

A couple of men skated toward them quickly.
One of them was Mr. Farmer, Joe's dad. He
helped Jimmie to his feet.

"You okay, Jimmie?" he asked anxiously.

"Yes," replied Jimmic. But when he skated
away he was moving very carefully.

Mr. Farmer turned to Tod. He looked pro-
voked. "Better be more careful next time, Tod,
or you'd better put your hockey stick and puck
away. That goes for the rest of you boys, too."

Tod's face reddened. He skated to the puck
and picked it up. He carried it back to the
small area where Skip and the others were waiting for him. Skip looked really angry.

"You nut," he said. "Why didn't you watch
where you were going?"

Tod said nothing. He felt like going home
then and there. Instead, he dropped the puck,
and this time they were all more careful about
their passes.

18

It didn't turn out to be as much fun as before, so Skip and Tim laid their hockey sticks aside and just skated. Tod didn't mind. Now he, Joe and Jack had the puck to themselves.

"Tod," Joe said, "I never see your dad here. Doesn't he skate?"

The question made Tod flush up a little. "No," he said. "He used to ski, but he hasn't for a long time."

Tod took a deep breath, spun halfway around, skated backwards a little ways and came to a quick stop. "I'm tired," he said. "Think I'll go home."

"There's no school tomorrow," reminded Joe. "Bring your puck, and we'll practice passing and dribbling. Okay?"

"Okay," agreed Tod.

He called to Jane, and she was willing to go home with him. They put on their boots and trudged back through the snow.

They reached the country road and stamped the snow off their boots. A snowplow had cleared the road and left high banks of the white powdery stuff on both sides.

Tod and Jane walked past Biff Jones's house and saw the Jones's Christmas tree through the large picture window. *Wonder what Biff will get for Christmas?* he thought.

Just a short distance farther on was their own home. It was a good one hundred feet from the road. A white house with blue shutters, with the English-style letter "B" cut in them. Dad had made them himself.

The front door looked very pretty with the big white cane on it and a red bow tied on the cane. The Christmas tree in the picture window looked very pretty, too. Even from outdoors you could see how broad it was. The big round bulbs and the hanging tinsels glinted like stars where the sun hit them.

Tod's heart warmed, and he smiled.

"What would you like best of all for Christmas, Jane?" he asked quietly.

"A bicycle," she said. "A small two-wheeler. What would you like?"

"I won't say," he answered. "I'll just wait and see if I get it."

3

IT WAS CHRISTMAS morning.
Tod and Jane came out of their bedrooms
in their pajamas. Jane ran, screaming happily,
for there beside the tree was exactly what she
had been wishing for—a sparkling red and
white bicycle.

Tod didn't run. He used to run when he was

Jane's age. But he was older now. Anyway, his long steps got him there fast enough.

There were big boxes and small boxes piled under the tree, all in fancy wrapping paper and fancy bows. There were also presents that were not wrapped — games, puzzles and books for him and Jane. These were the gifts Santa Claus had brought. Tod knew all about that little fat man in the bright red suit and white whiskers. But Jane didn't. Not everything, anyway.

And then he saw the really long gift wrapped beautifully in white and green paper with a wide red ribbon tied around it. His heart thumped, and he let out a yell as he ran toward it. Just to make sure that the present was his, though, he looked at the small tag tied to it.

For Tod, from Mom and Dad.

It was *it!* He just knew it was!

He tore the beautiful wrapping paper off and there it was. A hockey stick!

He tested its weight. Perfect! He laid the blade against the floor to test its lie. Perfect! He

ran his hands up and down its smooth polished surface. Perfect! Everything about it was just *perfect*.

Jane turned from her bicycle and ran toward the door. Mom and Dad were standing just in front of the doorway, wearing their bathrobes and smiling joyfully.

Jane flung her arms around them, and they bent forward and kissed her. Then Tod walked over to them, carrying his hockey stick.

"Thanks, Dad. Thanks, Mom," he said, and gave them both a tight hug. He wasn't able to say anything else. Something in his throat felt ready to burst.

It was a long while later — after they had opened all their presents and given Mom and Dad theirs — when Tod said, "Can I put some tape on it, Dad, and take it to the pond this afternoon?"

"Of course," said Dad. "That's what it's for."

Tod's face was as bright as one of the bulbs on the Christmas tree. "I'll show them when I get on that ice," he said proudly. "You wait and see." He looked up at his dad, eagerness sparkling in his eyes. "You're coming to our game Saturday morning, aren't you, Dad? We're scrimmaging against the Trojans."

Dad looked at him and shook his head disappointedly. "You know I can't, Tod. I have to be at the department."

"Oh, that's right," said Tod. "Then you won't be able to see any game, will you?"

Dad ruffled his hair. "Maybe I can make an arrangement to get away once or twice," he said. "We'll see."

Dad worked at the Fire Department. His days off were Sundays and Mondays.

"Will you put the tape on it for me, please, Dad?" asked Tod.

"Sure will," said Dad.

They went downstairs into the basement where Dad had a small workshop. Tod took his old, beat-up hockey stick with him for Dad to copy from.

While Dad was wrapping the tape around the blade of the new hockey stick, Tod remembered what Joe Farmer had asked him at the ice pond.

"You used to ski, didn't you, Dad?"

"Yes, I used to ski. Why?"

Tod shrugged. "Well, I remembered Mom saying you did. Was that before you and Mom were married?"

Dad's eyes lifted to Tod's and then returned to his task. "Yes. I skied for a long time, Tod. Started when I was a child, as you with your skating. Got to be fairly good, too. Then I injured my knee and had to give it up."

He shrugged, smiled. He was finished taping the blade of the hockey stick.

"There you are, son. Ready for action."

"Thanks, Dad. Mind if I go to the pond now?"

"Better wait till after lunch," suggested Dad. "That roast beef smells as if it's almost ready to sink our teeth into."

Tod spent almost two hours at the ice pond. Skip, Snowball, Tim and some other kids were there, too. They admired Tod's new hockey stick. Tod's face beamed with pride as he saw the looks of envy come over their faces. Without a doubt he had the nicest and best hockey stick of them all.

The crowd that assembled at the ice ponddid not make it possible for the boys to play scrub, so they just passed the puck and dribbled. Tod realized that his passes were better. He dribbled better, too.

At least, he thought so.

Then came Saturday and the scrimmage game with the Trojans at Manna Rink. Mr. Farmer, Joe's dad, was at the timekeeper's bench. The game would be played with exactly the same rules as a regular league game. In the Bantam League the teams played two 20-minute periods, not three as in college or professional hockey; high school teams played three 15-minute periods. Line 1 played two 4-

minute sessions and Lines 2 and 3 two 3-minute sessions each during each period.

Line 1 of both teams was out on the rink, ready for the referee to drop the puck. The White Knights wore white suits with black trim and the Trojans orange suits with blue and white trim. Their legs looked chubby with shin guards under their long stockings. Sweaters, with stripes on the sleeves and large numbers on the back and small on the front, covered their padded shoulders and elbows. The pants were padded, too. And they all wore padded gloves.

The goalies were especially protected. They wore face masks, chest protectors, huge padded leg guards and extra-padded goal gloves. The blades of the goal sticks were larger than those used by the other players. Because the sticks received a lot of pounding, they were taped over the heel and partway up the shaft.

Every player wore a helmet. Most of the helmets were of different colors because they were owned by the players. They weren't turned in to the league at the end of the season as the uniforms were.

For a moment there was complete silence. Then the referee dropped the puck in the center circle of the ice. The game was on.

Joe Farmer, center, grabbed the puck and passed to his right wingman, Eddie Jones. A Trojan player swept in and intercepted the pass. He dribbled it across the neutral zone, crossed the White Knights' blue line and headed for the net.

Both defensemen, Al Burns and Duck Franks, went after him. Goalie Jim Smith was crouched, waiting tensely.

Al Burns reached the Trojan first. Al tried to steal the puck and hooked the blade of his stick with the Trojans'. Another Trojan poke-checked the puck and sent it rolling across the ice toward the boards. Duck Franks sped up to it and drove it back up the ice toward Trojans' territory.

30

Joe Farmer had it for a while, dribbling toward the Trojans' goal. He snapped a shot at it, but the goalie stopped it with his heavy pads for a save and then cleared it away from the net with his stick.

"Be ready, Line 2," said Coach Fillis. He was leaning against the boards in front of the bench where his boys were sitting. In his hand was a clipboard with the roster of the White Knights fastened to it. "Let's see you snap one into that net."

A short time later the buzzer sounded. Line 1 of both teams hurried off the ice, and Line 2 hurried on. Quickly they moved into their positions: Skip Haddock at center, Tod at right forward, Jim Wright at left forward. Behind them at right defense was Biff Jones, at left defense Snowball Harry Carr, and goalie Tim Collins.

Pete Sunday, the Trojans' star center, got the puck away from Skip and passed it to a wingman. Tod moved up quickly, his pumping legs

31

sending chips flying from the blades of his skates. In his hand was the brand new hockey stick, the light twinkling on its shiny surface. This was the moment he had been waiting for. Now he could show what he could do.

Someone bumped into the Trojan wingman and the puck skittered away, free. A mad scramble for it followed. Snowball went down and a Trojan player fell on top of him.

Skip got the puck and started with it across the red line in the center of the rink. Two Trojans came after him and he passed to Tod. Tod caught it and dribbled it across the Trojans' blue line. He felt so good he could smile. A Trojan defenseman was coming at him, but he didn't care. Tod knew he could out-skate him. And with his new hockey stick he could push that puck wherever he pleased.

He stepped up his speed and gave the puck an extra shove.

Too far! For a second his heart jumped to his

throat. He caught up with the puck just before the Trojan player did and tried to glide it lightly ahead of him.

Again too far! He tried to catch up with it, but another Trojan player swept in and took control of it. It was Pete Sunday.

"Thanks, Tod, ol' buddy," said Pete, and started to dribble the puck back up the ice, skating close to the boards.

Tod's skates shrieked and shot a stream of ice chips as he came to a stop and bolted back up the ice after Pete. His face was hot as Pete's words rang in his ears.

He came up behind Pete, tried to poke-check the puck. His skate tangled with Pete's, and down Tod went. He heard Pete laugh as the Trojan center dribbled the puck toward the White Knights' net.

Quickly, Tod rose to his feet and raced after Pete and the puck. Snowball was already there, trying to take the puck. His stick and Pete's sounded like cracking whips as they smacked against each other.

Then Skip got there — just a fraction of a second before Tod did — and struck Pete with a body-check. Pete lost control of the puck, and Skip hooked it with the blade of his stick. Pete charged hard toward Skip, and Tod yelled:

"Here, Skip!"

Skip passed to him. The puck sped like a black bullet. Tod went after it, stuck out his stick.

Missed it! The puck sailed past. Tod, clamping his lips together, whirled and went after it. A Trojan went after it, too. They would meet the puck at the same time.

Tod reached out with his stick. It barely touched the puck.

Tod was so anxious to get the puck that he forgot about the Trojan charging after it, too. They collided solidly. The breath was knocked out of him for an instant, and he fell to the ice.

Another orange player came racing toward him.

Tod looked hastily around, saw the puck inches away. He started to swing his stick toward it while still on his knees. Just as he swung the Trojan tripped over the stick and went flying forward on his face, skidding almost fifteen feet before he stopped.

A whistle shrilled. Tod paid little attention to it. He got to his feet and dug his skates into the ice, racing after the puck that had been hit toward the boards.

Shreeek! Shreeek! went the whistle again.

"Hold it, Tod!" shouted a voice.

Tod slowed and turned around. The referee was skating swiftly toward the puck.

"Tripping!" he said, touching Tod on the shoulder as he went by. Then he gathered up the puck and skated toward the scorekeeper's bench to inform the scorekeeper of the penalty.

Tod's heart sank. Taking hold of his stick with both hands, he skated slowly off the ice.

"Hurry it up!" snapped the referee.

Tod's neck reddened. He hurried off the ice to the penalty box.

"One minute, Tod," said Mr. Farmer.

It seemed a long time before the end of that minute came.

"Okay, Tod, get in there, quick," Mr. Farmer told him.

Tod got hurriedly back on the ice. But less than thirty seconds later the buzzer sounded, and Line 2 skated off.

After a minute or so Line 3 for the Trojans managed to drive one past the White Knights' goalie for a score. When the White Knights' Line 1 returned to the ice, they tried their best to tie it up, but it was their Line 2 that finally did it. Skip made the goal with Biff getting credit for an assist. Tod did no better during that session than he had the first time.

"You're a little tight out there," said the coach during the intermission. "Keep your hands farther apart. And hit that puck a little easier. Don't look so glum. You'll do all right."

But when Line 2 went in for their turn after intermission, Tod didn't do all right. He missed two passes completely.

There was more scoring this period, with Skip and Snowball sharing two apiece and Biff getting three assists.

The game tied up in the last two minutes. And then the Trojans socked one past Goalie Tim Collins for a beautiful shot that put them ahead. That was the way the game ended, Trojans — 6; White Knights — 5.

All the way home Tod hardly said a word. He was thinking. He had supposed that a brand-new hockey stick would make him play better hockey. He had learned today that this wasn't so. He didn't think he deserved that new hockey stick at all.

Even at home he thought and thought about it. And then he knew what he would do. He would put his new hockey stick away. He wouldn't play with it again until he felt, deep in his heart, that he deserved it.

He stuck it inside the closet of his room. No matter how much he liked it, he wouldn't play with it again until he played a lot better than he did today.

4

THE WHITE KNIGHTS' first league game
was against the Trojans, the same team they
had scrimmaged with last Saturday. The game
was at ten o'clock in the morning.

Tod sat on the bench between Biff and Snowball. In his hand was the old hockey stick. The
shine had been gone a long time ago. The bot-

tom of the blade was worn and splintered. Even part of the tape was worn off.

A real crummy-looking stick. But it wasn't the stick that made a good hockey player. It was the hockey player himself. Tod knew that now.

He watched the game, and every once in a while he glanced at the clock. The flashing red dots spelled out the seconds that were left.

Neither team looked as if it were going to do any scoring this session. Passes were poor, and both teams had off-sides called on them. The players who had the puck in their possession seemed to forget that they couldn't cross the blue line into the attacking zone before the puck did.

The buzzer sounded, and Line 2 took over. Again facing Skip at the center spot was Pete Sunday. Pete had practically won the game by himself last Saturday. This was the boy the White Knights had to watch out for.

Tod, playing right wing, caught the puck as it flashed across the ice to him. He started to

40

move it across the red line, saw a Trojan player coming at him, and passed to Skip. But he struck the puck too hard. It whizzed by Skip, and both Skip and Biff chased after it.

Tod skated down center ice as fast as his legs could go. He had made up his mind to play good hockey. It was the only way he could gain back that hockey stick that stood resting in the dark corner of his clothes closet.

Biff reached the puck and shot it across the ice to Tod. Just as Tod caught it with his stick two Trojan players arrived on the spot, too. One of them body-checked Tod, knocking him away from the puck. Before he realized it, the puck was sliding a mile a minute up toward the other end of the rink. It went past the goal line and both referees raised their right arms, ready to blow their whistles.

Biff reached the puck first, struck it with his stick, and the whistles shrilled.

"Icing!" shouted one of the referees.

Face-off in the wide ring to the left of the

41

goal. The mad scramble for the puck. Down went Snowball Harry Carr in a spill.

Tod grinned. Snowball had been doing well so far. This was the first time he had fallen.

A few seconds later Pete Sunday tapped in the puck for a goal.

Biff tied it up with an assist by Snowball.

Later, Snowball golfed one into the net, but Pete Sunday tied it up again, 2-2.

Tod worked hard to play better hockey, but the harder he tried the worse he seemed to get. He even fell a few times, a thing he seldom did. He knew it was because he was too anxious, but he couldn't help it.

And then it was Line 2's last time on the ice. Tod raced with a Trojan after the puck as it headed for the corner in the Trojans' end zone.

Both players kept their heads down, speeding as fast as their legs could go. *Zup-zup! Zup-zup!* sang their skates. Tod tightened his lips. The Trojan was beating him to the puck!

The Trojan reached it first. Unable to stop,

stick swinging wild, Tod ran into him. The Trojan banged against the boards with a sound that echoed throughout the huge building.

Shree-e-ek! The referee's whistle pierced the rink.

"Charging! Lifting the stick too high!"

Tod's face turned a beet red. "But I didn't mean —"

"Two minutes in the penalty box!" snapped the referee.

His head hanging down, Tod skated sadly off the ice. For a split second he glanced up and saw Mr. Farmer and Mr. Haddock looking directly at him.

"That's dangerous raising your stick like that," Mr. Farmer said.

Tod looked away, pulling himself through the doorway into the penalty box, and sat down. His neck was burning.

5

TOD WAS SICK. Two minutes! Line 2
would be off the ice about the time those
two minutes were up.

He sat back unhappily and watched the
White Knights play ice hockey with four men
against five. He knew that lifting the stick too
high was a penalty. But he hadn't realized he
was doing it. He had tried to keep himself from

45

striking the Trojan player with his body by protecting himself with his hands. He hadn't even thought about the stick.

Once . . . twice . . . the White Knights shot the puck all the way down the ice and past the Trojans' goal. With only four men playing, the White Knights were allowed to do that. They fought hard to keep the puck in the attacking zone.

And then Skip had the puck, dribbling it fast behind the Trojans' net. He swung in front of the goal and gave the puck a snap. Like a dart it flashed into the net!

Just after the face-off, Tod heard a shout behind him. "Okay, Baker! Get back in there!"

Tod climbed over the boards onto the ice. He raced after the puck which was being poked at by two Trojans and a White Knights player. The puck rolled freely for a moment, and Tod reached it. He dribbled it a bit, saw a Trojan heading fast toward him, and looked around for someone to pass to.

Biff was just inside the blue line, in the neutral zone. Tod passed the puck to him. Biff caught it with his stick, dribbled it across the blue line and then passed to Skip.

That was as far as the puck went. The buzzer sounded, and Line 2 skated off the ice.

Line 3 made no change in the score. The game ended with the White Knights capturing their first league game, 3-2.

"Nice game, boys," Coach Fillis said happily in the locker room as the boys changed their skates for shoes. "Every one of you did a bang-up job. Make sure you practice during the week. Wish we could have this rink to practice on, but we can't. See you next Saturday!"

Ms. Hudson, Tod's fifth-grade teacher, looked through her tortoiseshell glasses at the pupils in her room.

"We're going to have tests tomorrow," she said. "In arithmetic, social studies and English. They will be on subjects we have studied during the past few weeks. I think there are some of you who had better review those subjects with special care. It seems that there are some students who pay more attention to outside activities than they do to their studies."

Her eyes met Tod's, and his face turned red. She looked at the next pupil, but he knew she had been referring to him and several other boys who played ice hockey.

He studied all he could that day. When school was over he carried his books home and reviewed things they had worked on since Christmas vacation and a few weeks before. He asked Mom and Dad to help him on questions he couldn't understand, and they did. He didn't go to the ice pond at all that evening.

The next day Ms. Hudson gave them the tests and on Wednesday she returned the papers to them.

When she handed Tod's to him, he saw that one paper had a mark in the top 80's. The other two were in the 70's.

"I know you must have studied hard Monday evening for yesterday's tests, Tod," she said. "But you can't expect to review everything in one night and remember it all. Seems to me you're spending more time than necessary with something less important than your schoolwork. Education, you know, is more important than basketball."

"Hockey," he corrected her. "Not basketball."

She smiled just a little. "Okay. Hockey."

He knew then and there that he would have little chance of becoming a good hockey player if she had her way. Of course, he had to study. But he had to practice, too. How could he expect to play well enough to deserve that brand-new hockey stick that stood in the closet if he didn't practice?

Tod laid his face in his hands. A guy could not expect to get anyplace in sports if his teacher was a sports hater. And that's what Ms. Hudson was.

A sports hater.

6

THE LOCKER ROOM was a den of excitement. Boys in White Knights and Vikings uniforms were sitting side by side on the benches, putting on their skates.

Tod spotted Jack Evans lacing his skate shoes. A strange feeling came over him. Last year he and Jack played on the same team. This year Jack was wearing a Vikings uniform. He was playing against Tod, not with him.

Tod didn't know whether he should sit beside Jack or not. Then Jack's eyes lifted. They met Tod's, and a warm smile came over Jack's face.

"Hi, Tod!" he said. "What line are you playing on?"

"Line 2," replied Tod. "What line are you on?"

"Two, too!" Jack laughed. "That's something, isn't it? Us playing against each other this year?"

"That's what I was thinking," said Tod.

He sat beside Jack and took off his shoes. They talked about their games played last week. The Vikings had tied with the Spartans, 2-2.

"I made both goals," smiled Jack. "How are you doing, Tod?"

Tod's face dropped. "Not good," he said.

Coach Fillis entered the room. He came over to Tod.

"Tod, I'm going to try you at right defense today. Okay?"

Tod looked up. His face flushed a little. He didn't want to play a defensive position. Defensemen had to play the zone in front of their goal most of the time. They had to help their goalie protect the net from the attacking forwards of the other team. Of course, it was important. But it wasn't what Tod liked. Forwards could skate all over the rink at all times, so long as they kept in balance with the other members of their line. That's what he preferred. But he couldn't argue with the coach.

"Okay, Mr. Fillis," he said.

"Good," said Coach Fillis. "Better get out there and loosen up. The game will be starting soon."

He and Jack walked out together. They got on the ice and joined the dozens of players who were already on it. They skated round and round, forward and backward, bending their knees, twisting to the left and right.

Finally the whistle blew. Everyone skated off the ice except Line 1 of both teams.

A little while later the teams were lined up. The referee stood ready with the puck in his hand and the whistle in his mouth. Then the whistle shrilled, he dropped the puck, and the game was on.

Tod's heart pounded as if he were right there on the ice with Line 1. Both teams were skating strong, fighting for control of the puck. Sticks clashed. Skates swished. The Vikings became overexcited. Two players skated over the White Knights' blue line before their man passed the puck to them, and a face-off was called for off-sides.

A few moments later Eddie Jones took a pass from Larry Thomas, went over the Vikings' blue line and drove hard for the net. Tod watched Eddie jealously. He was pushing that puck along in front of him swiftly and with ease—and Eddie was a year younger than he! Of course there was a reason for Eddie's being so good. His dad was a good skater, too. He had worked out with Eddie almost since Eddie was old enough to put on skates. Well, maybe not that long—but pretty long.

Eddie swung up beside the Vikings' net and shot the puck. It struck the goalie's shin guard and bounced back. Then Larry came up, picked up the puck on rebound and poked it in.

Goal!

A rousing cheer sprang from the White Knights' bench. Tod couldn't help but beat his old hockey stick against the boards, too, as the others were doing.

Then it was Line 2's turn. Tod skated to the defense position, working with Snowball. Snowball yelled at him, and his pie-shaped face spread into a big grin.

"Just let them try to get past us! Huh, Toddy, boy?"

"Yeah," said Tod, rather meekly.

Face-off. Again the puck became a jumping, skittering, flying black dot. Skip soon took it into the clear, passing it to Bud Wooley, who was playing right forward today. Bud took it, passed it back. Someone swept in like a blue streak, intercepted the puck and passed it to another player in blue.

Seconds later Tod saw Jack Evans coming down center ice. There was some passing, but Jack ended up with the puck and swung around behind the White Knights' goal with it.

Tod watched the play closely but nervously. It was hard to believe that a good friend of his like Jack was playing against him. Now there was Jack coming at him with the puck. Tod made a jab at it with his stick but missed. Jack turned his body, struck Tod with his hip and swung around Tod with the puck still in his possession.

One split second later Jack flicked his stick and the puck flashed straight over Goalie Tim

Collins's wide stick into the net.

Tod's jaw dropped. A shoulder brushed roughly against him. He looked around and met Skip's angry eyes.

"You on our side or theirs?" snarled Skip. "Get your body into it. Check him."

The remark stung. Tod was glad when the whistle blew and they got off the ice.

Snowball patted him comfortingly on the shoulder. "That's okay, Toddy. We'll stop 'em the next time."

The seconds ticked away rapidly on the electric scoreboard. The Vikings scored another goal, and for a while they skated with lots of pride and confidence.

When Line 2 went back in, Jack Evans had the puck most of the time. Tod didn't know just what to do when Jack dribbled the puck toward him, almost daring Tod to try to steal the puck from him.

Tod jabbed halfheartedly at the puck. He

could have gone after it hard, fought for it. But he didn't.

Jack took off like a flash and dribbled past Tod. A few seconds later he scored another goal.

"Come on, Tod! Get in there!" came a shout from the sideline. "Take that puck from him. You're playing defense. Use your body as well as your stick."

It was Coach Fillis's voice.

He heard other remarks. From Skip and Biff. Yes, even from Biff, who was his neighbor.

But they're right, he thought. *I am too easy with Jack. And I shouldn't be. Just as he isn't easy with me.*

He made up his mind to play differently. The next time Jack came toward him with the puck, Tod forgot about how friendly they were. He dug his skates hard into the ice and went after the puck as if his life depended on it.

Ice chips flew up against him as Jack tried to spin away from him. Tod's stick hooked Jack's,

57

and for a couple of seconds their sticks were locked together. Tod looked up, met Jack's eyes, saw the surprise in them.

Sorry, Jack! But I'm here to play as hard as I can, too! he thought.

Then his stick broke loose from Jack's, and he knocked the puck away.

Later, he did it again. He and Jack were real opponents now.

Jack didn't score another goal.

The White Knights won the close game, 5-4. As they skated off the ice, Jack smiled at Tod. "Nice game, Tod!" he said.

"Thanks!" said Tod. "You, too, Jack!"

7

IN THE LOCKER room, Skip picked up the old hockey stick that was leaning on the bench beside Tod.

"What happened to the new stick you had, Tod?"

Tod blushed. His shoes were laced. He was ready to leave for home.

"It's home," he said, rising from the bench.

"Home?" Skip echoed. "What's it doing there?"

Tod shrugged. "Nothing."

"That's right," said Biff. "You had a new one at the ice pond, didn't you? What're you saving it for?"

"This one has a lot of wear in it yet," said Tod.

He was anxious to go. He didn't want to talk about his new hockey stick. No one had a right to know why he didn't want to play with it.

"This stick is really beat-up," said Skip. He turned it over and pointed at the worn tape and the marred-up blade. "Look at that. Cracked and everything. And you say it has a lot of wear in it yet? You're nuts, Tod."

"Okay, I'm nuts," said Tod. He took the stick away from Skip. "See you out by the car, Biff. So long, Jack."

He walked out, feeling their eyes on his back. He was sweating, and it wasn't warm at all in the locker room.

The next Saturday morning, at eleven o'clock, the White Knights played the Spartans.

The Spartans were colorful in their red suits with white trim. Their scoring ace was Cliff Towne. But today he did not seem to be the master of the puck he usually was. Cliff was center on the Spartans' Line 2, and he and Skip were playing about even.

Tod, waiting for Line 2's turn on the ice for the second time, spotted a familiar face in a seat on the other side. It was a man dressed in a black sweater with two stripes around the chest. He was blond-haired, and he looked very much like Mr. Porter, the physical education teacher at the school.

"Isn't that Mr. Porter?" Tod asked Biff.

Biff looked. "You're right! It is! Wonder who that woman is with him?"

"I don't know," said Tod.

The woman with Mr. Porter had a white hat on, a milk-white sweater and black jeans. It was hard to see her from here.

Then Tod forgot about Mr. Porter and the woman and concentrated on the game.

Both teams played recklessly. There was a lot of passing, but the receivers were seldom in the right position to receive the puck. Skaters collided and fell sprawling over each other on the ice.

When Line 2 replaced Line 1, they did not perform any better. Snowball fell so often that he seemed to be sitting on the ice more times than he was skating on it. This was just a bad day for the White Knights — and for the Spartans, too. Tod could hear the few spectators laughing loudly in the seats as if they were watching a three-ring circus.

Just before Line 2 was to return to the ice for the last time, Tod looked across the rink. The seats where he had seen Mr. Porter and the woman sitting were empty.

Tod thought of the brand-new hockey stick

resting in the corner of his closet. Maybe he was wrong in making such a strong promise. Maybe he should break it. No one knew why he wasn't using that new stick. He could take it and play with it in the next game. At least he'd get some fun out of it before the season was over with.

Anyway, how could he know when he was playing good enough hockey to feel that he deserved the new hockey stick?

He'd get it and play with it, that's what he'd do.

But the next instant he changed his mind again. No. He had made a promise to himself. IIe would stick to it.

Through practicing and hard work he'd make himself be a better hockey player. He just had to.

When Line 2 got on the ice Tod tried as hard as he could to play better hockey. At face-off, Skip grabbed the puck from Cliff Towne and passed it to Jim Wright. Jim dribbled across the neutral zone toward the Spartans' blue line and

63

shot the puck across the ice toward Bud Wooley.
Bud missed it.

Two Spartans dashed after it. Tod saw that
one of them was certain to intercept the puck.
Quickly, he dug his skates into the ice and
sprang forward, his head down and his stick
clutched in both hands.

A Spartan appeared like a streak beside him.
His skate caught Tod's for an instant. Tod almost lost his balance. He shoved the player
aside with a swing of his hip and lowered his
stick to stop the puck. As he did so, he was
bumped hard by the other Spartan. *Crash!*

Every bone in his body was jarred by the im-
pact. He wobbled and struggled hard to keep
from falling. Dazedly, he looked around for the
puck. He saw it, skidding across the Spartans'
blue line only a couple of feet away.

The Spartan shoved him aside in trying to get
at the puck. If he got it, he could shoot it back
out of his zone. But the puck was in a good spot
for the White Knights to score.

Maybe I can break the 0-0 tie, myself! thought Tod.

Like a fighting rooster Tod shook away from the Spartan and bolted after the puck. Just then he saw Jim and another Spartan player charge after it together. The Spartan's stick reached out, hooked the puck.

For a fraction of a second Tod's hopes drained. Then he lashed out his stick. Instead of striking the puck, the blade caught inside the Spartan's left skate. Down went the Spartan!

Shree-e-ek!

"Tripping!" shouted the referee.

Tod stared at him. His mouth fell open, but he said nothing. He took a deep breath and skated off the ice toward the penalty box.

He had tried hard — and had committed a foul. Of course it was his fault. He knew that. He just wasn't thinking when he had swung that stick.

It just proved, more than ever, that he didn't deserve that new hockey stick.

65

Seconds before Line 2's time was up, Jim shot the puck to Skip near the Spartans' goal crease. Skip caught it with the flat of his stick, turned around quickly and gave the puck a snap.

Past the goalie's leg guards it sailed for a goal!

Line 3 could do nothing. The game ended, 1-0 in favor of the White Knights.

The boys had mixed feelings as they left Manna Rink. Some were very happy about the win. They had forgotten about how poorly they had played. Others, especially Tod, were not as happy. They had played a terrible game. They said that the score should be 8-0, not 1-0.

Around three o'clock, Tod and Jane went to the ice pond. Several skaters were already there. Matter of fact, two of them were the same two Tod had seen at Manna Rink — Mr. Porter and the woman.

"Hi, Mr. Porter!" he yelled.

"Well, hi, Tod! Hi, Jane!"

And then the woman with Mr. Porter looked at them, too.

"Hello!" she yelled to them. She was skating so well, Tod thought, that she must be some professional whom Mr. Porter knew.

And then he recognized her, and his mouth popped open. He could scarcely believe his eyes.

"Why, it's Ms. Hudson!"

It really was! Ms. Hudson, his fifth-grade teacher, whom he had figured as a sports hater! She looked so different without glasses and in that sweater and jeans!

She laughed. "Yes, it's me! Surprised?"

Tod gulped. "Surprised? Yes! Yes, I am! I never dreamed I'd see you here!"

8

M R. PORTER AND Ms. Hudson skated to the bench where Tod and Jane stopped to put on their skates. Ms. Hudson's cheeks were apple-red from the cold. Her brown eyes flashed like washed walnuts.

"Why not?" she asked Tod.

Tod stared at her. "I thought you hated skating," he said. "I thought you hated all kinds of sports."

"Me?" Ms. Hudson's eyes opened wide. "Whatever gave you that idea?" And then her expression changed, as if she remembered something. "Oh, yes! I know now. Some time ago I warned a certain boy that his studies were more important than basketball."

Tod grinned. "Hockey," he said.

She smiled. So did Mr. Porter. "Yes. Hockey," she said, and laughed.

"Don't let her kid you, Tod," said Mr. Porter. "She knows the difference all right. We saw you play this morning, you know."

"Yes. I saw you," said Tod. "A lousy game, wasn't it?"

"Well — it's pretty early in the season," said Mr. Porter. "You boys will improve plenty as the season grows older. Hurry. Get your skates on. We'll see you on the ice!"

Jane and Tod put on their skates and stepped out onto the ice.

"Wow!" exclaimed Jane. "Look at Ms. Hudson skate, Tod! She's marvelous!"

Tod stopped and looked at Ms. Hudson as if he were seeing things. There she was, skating backward as if she had eyes behind her head. She was moving with terrific speed, her body leaning forward, her legs bent and driving strongly. Suddenly she balanced on her right foot alone and stretched her left leg gracefully straight out behind her.

"How do you like that?" cried Tod. "And I thought she hated sports!"

Jane chuckled. "She certainly fooled you, didn't she?" she said, and took off like a blown leaf across the ice.

They remained on the pond for almost two hours. Ms. Hudson and Jane skated together most of the time, holding each other's hands while they skated frontward and backward. Tod saw that Jane was having a lot of fun. Several other skaters stopped and watched them. Indeed, Ms. Hudson was one of the best

skaters who had ever appeared on their ice pond.

It was practically a show she and Jane put on for them. When they were finished the people applauded.

Tod couldn't get over it. Ms. Hudson! His fifth-grade teacher — a skater like that!

Tod practiced dribbling and passing on the ice pond with Snowball, Skip and some of his other teammates during the week. He managed to do better with his studies, too. In school he just couldn't get over the sight of Ms. Hudson with her glasses on, looking so much — well, so much like a teacher. You wouldn't think *she'd* wear jeans and be able to figure skate so well.

In the game against the Trojans on January 26, Coach Fillis had Tod playing defense again. Tod tried his best to play his position but he just couldn't block his opponents with his body or intercept the puck with his hockey stick as well as he should. The Trojans scored two goals that they should not have, all because Tod couldn't keep the man from dribbling past him as he swung around from behind the net. Both times the Trojan skated up in front of the net and sent the puck blazing past Tim's shin pads.

In the second period Coach Fillis didn't play Tod at all. The coach had Bud Wooley substitute for him. Tod sat on the bench and watched the remainder of the game with his heart hurting as it had never hurt before. This was the first time he had missed playing. And he deserved it. He knew he did. He wasn't playing good hockey at all.

"Cheer up, Toddy, ol' buddy," said Snowball as Line 2 came off the ice the first time that second period. "Look how many times I've been down. And I still get up. Don't take it so hard. That's the way I look at it."

"I guess that's the best way," said Tod gloomily.

73

But you don't have a brand-new hockey stick resting in a closet at home, he thought. *You don't really care about whether you deserve to play with a new hockey stick or not. I made a promise I'd never play with that stick until I deserved it. And I have to do as I promised myself. You don't know that, Snowball. You don't know that I had wanted that hockey stick more than anything else in this world, and now that I have it I can't play with it because of that promise.*

Never make a promise like that, Snowball. Never.

9

THE WHITE KNIGHTS were losing, 4-3. They were receiving their first setback of the season.

Skip Haddock was having a field day of penalties. He was sent to the penalty box twice — once for body-checking a man against the boards, and again for lifting his stick too high and, in doing so, striking an opponent.

No one on the ice played harder than Skip. He was certainly anxious to pull the game out of the fire for the White Knights.

Tod watched him admiringly. Even Coach Fillis remarked about him.

But Skip's pluck and energy weren't enough. The White Knights fell victim to the Trojans 4-3.

In the locker room Coach Fillis praised Skip for his pluckiness, but reminded him about his penalties. "I don't like unnecessary roughness," he said. "You can always play good, fast hockey without roughing it up. And a high stick in a scramble might tear open a boy's face. Remember that, every one of you."

He also pointed out Tod's mistakes. They were no different than before. Tod was a speedster on skates, said the coach, but he still wasn't able to stickhandle correctly. He still needed more practice. Especially in passing.

Practice, thought Tod unhappily. *Probably*

I practice more than anyone else on the team now.

"I think you do better as a wingman, anyway, Tod," said Coach Fillis. "You can get to the puck faster than almost anyone else on the team. That's really important. I'm sure that as time goes on you'll make out fine."

Tod thought of the coach's kind words as he rode home with Biff. Mr. Fillis was really a fine guy. He didn't "chew you out" for not playing well. He usually understood the reasons and tried to offer criticism that would help you.

Biff's voice interrupted Tod's thoughts. "Doesn't your father like hockey, Tod? I've never seen him at our games."

"He has to work Saturday mornings," explained Tod.

"Oh, that's right. He's a fireman, isn't he?"

Tod nodded. "Yes."

Mr. Jones looked aside at Tod as he stopped at a red signal. "I heard that there are plans for a Father and Son Banquet to be held soon, Tod. It's going to be at the Packer Hotel for all the hockey players and their dads. Think your dad would like to go to it?"

Tod shrugged. "Probably."

"I think he would," said Mr. Jones, moving the car forward again as the light turned green. "Don't forget to ask him, anyway. I'm sure there are lots of other dads who would like to meet him."

Tod didn't answer. Dad wouldn't care about going to any Father and Son Banquet. He hardly knew any of the other dads and he wouldn't especially care to make new acquaintances. No, he wouldn't say a thing about it to Dad.

"Hey, Dad," said Biff. "I heard there's going to be an Ice Show coming up, too. Have you heard anything about it?"

"Yes, I heard about that, too. Matter of fact, Tom Welling, the fellow who directs our hockey program, told me a few days ago that plans have already been arranged."

"Great! Are they going to get someone like the Ice Follies?" asked Biff.

"No. They're going to get people from around town here. Seems that there are enough excellent skaters nearby who can put on a good show, too."

"I bet Ms. Hudson will be in it," said Biff. "You've seen her skate, haven't you, Tod? She's terrific."

Tod nodded. "She's the best I've seen around here," he agreed.

Thinking of her made him forget his sad thoughts and he almost smiled. Ms. Hudson on skates. He certainly would never forget her as long as he lived.

Tod knew there was exciting news the moment he entered the house. Mom's face was lit up bright as a candle, and Jane's round face looked even brighter. Her big blue eyes were like brilliant moons. She began clapping her hands and dancing on her toes as if whatever was making her happy just couldn't keep.

Tod closed the door behind him and looked from Mom's face to Jane's. "Did somebody win a million dollars?"

Mom chuckled. "Not quite," she said. "Tell him, Jane."

"I'm going to be in the Ice Show!" she cried. "Isn't that wonderful?"

Tod stared. "We were just talking about the Ice Show!" he said. "Mr. Jones said there's going to be one. Who asked you?"

"Ms. Hudson," said Jane.

"Ms. Hudson? She's going to be in it, too?" Ms. Hudson seemed to be appearing in a lot of places lately.

"Yes. And she called Marylou Farmer, too. We're going to start practicing tomorrow afternoon at Manna Rink. Oh, I'm so thrilled!"

Just then a car drove into the yard. A few moments later Dad came in. He hardly had the door closed behind him before Jane rushed up to him and spilled the happy news.

Dad's lean face filled with pride. "When is the Ice Show?"

"February twentieth," replied Jane. "I'll be a wreck by then!"

Tod shook his head. You'd think Jane was in her teens the way she talked.

Dad removed his coat, cap and boots and started to put them away.

"Well, guess I'll have a chance, at least, to see my little girl skate," he said. "Hardly have a chance to see Tod do his stuff on skates. How did you make out this morning, son?"

"We lost," said Tod. "Four to three. It's just our first loss, though."

Dad ruffled his hair, smiled. "Don't be afraid to lose," he said. "Everyone loses sometime."

Tod remembered what Mr. Jones had said about the Father and Son Banquet. He looked at Dad. His lips parted. He almost mentioned the banquet to Dad, then changed his mind.

No, Dad wouldn't care about going. He didn't care about meeting the other dads. Anyway, he had a lot of work to do around the house . . . fixing the floors, the creaky steps. . . .

Dad turned and headed for the bathroom. Tod looked at Mom. She returned his look and smiled.

"As soon as Dad finishes, you'd better wash up, too," she said. "First, though, get out of that hockey uniform."

10

O N SUNDAY AFTERNOON Ms. Hudson
drove up in her old car and picked up Jane.
She had Marylou Farmer with her. Afterwards
Jane, in her breathless, excited way, told Dad,
Mom and Tod about all the men and women and
boys and girls who had been at Manna Rink to
practice for the coming Ice Show.

"Marylou and I are the youngest ones in the

83

whole show!" she said. "Isn't that unbelievable?"

"It sure is," replied Tod, and tried to keep from smiling.

Three nights a week — for almost an hour each time — Jane had to go to practice. Tod practiced hockey as much as he could at the ice pond, strengthening his leg muscles, improving his wind, trying body-checks, and above all, trying to get the feel of the puck on his hockey stick.

Then for two days the weather got so warm that he and all the other skaters were afraid that the ice would melt. However, the weather dipped to below zero after the second night, and their fears vanished.

Tod worked hard to improve his skill at stick-handling. He, Jack Evans and Biff Jones practiced together most of the time. He could play with those boys without feeling ashamed of his playing. Skip, Joe Farmer and some of the other guys were too good. He wasn't as comfortable practicing when they were around. They played with the puck mostly among themselves and gave him very few chances at passing.

On Saturday morning the White Knights played the eleven o'clock game against the Vikings. Coach Fillis had Tod back at the right wing spot, with Jim Wright at left wing and Skip at center. Biff and Snowball played in their defensive positions.

Tod was happy to be on the forward line again. He felt better playing forward. When you feel better at a certain position, you can play better. Tod knew he had to play much better if he ever hoped to use his new hockey stick. The season was moving along rapidly.

Skip scored the first goal for the White Knights. Twice Tod had an opportunity to slip the puck past the Viking goalie, but both times he failed. If he hadn't pushed the puck too hard . . .

But that was his main trouble, not being able to control the puck.

The score was 1-1 until fifteen seconds before

the end of Line 2's time on the ice. Then Jack Evans poked in a goal to put the Vikings in the lead 2 to 1.

The White Knights' Line 1 tied it up at the beginning of the second period. Joe Farmer scored with an assist by Larry Thomas.

"Okay, you guys," said Joe to the Line 2 players as Line 1 skated off the ice. "Let's see you break the tie."

"I'll break it," replied Skip.

Boy, thought Tod, *he doesn't think much of himself, does he?* From the second that the referee dropped the puck in the face-off, Skip was going to prove just what he said. He poke-checked the puck, gave Jack Evans a body-check that almost knocked him down, then had the puck to himself. He dribbled across the Vikings' blue line. Tod envied the way Skip stickhandled the puck. He did it so easily, guiding the puck as if it were magnetized to the hockey stick.

Then Jack Evans dashed up from behind

Skip. He shoved his stick under Skip's and stole the puck! In a flash Jack brought himself to a quick stop, ice chips flying from his skates. He turned and carried the puck back across the blue line, the red line, and then the White Knights' blue line.

Tod rushed him. Skip, who had skated back furiously, came at him from the other side. His leg shot in front of Jack and Jack stumbled and went down sprawling.

Shreeeek!

Time was called. The referee tapped Skip Haddock on the shoulder and pointed to the penalty box.

"I didn't mean it!" yelled Skip angrily.

The referee ignored him. He skated with Skip up to the timekeeper's desk. "Tripping!" he said. "One minute!"

Tod saw the burning look Skip gave the referee as he climbed over the boards to the bench instead of going through the door.

With their opponents having one less player, the Vikings worked harder than ever to break the tie. The White Knights fought even harder. Twenty seconds before Skip's time was up, Tod passed to Biff in front of the Vikings' net and Biff socked the puck in for a goal.

There, thought Tod. *At least I have one point, for an assist.* The one minute was up, and Skip returned to the ice. It was Line 3 that scored again for the White Knights, putting them in the lead 4 to 2.

Then, during the second time around, the Vikings got a good passing streak and knocked in two goals almost within a minute of each other. That was the best they could do, and the best that the White Knights could do, too. The game ended with a 4-4 tie.

In the locker room Jack Evans grinned at Tod and patted him on the shoulder. "Good game, Tod. You really looked great today."

Tod shrugged. "Thanks, Jack."

"You really did, Tod," said Coach Fillis, grinning. "You did a fine job of passing. Just keep that up."

A warm feeling went through Tod. Maybe those hard practices during the week were doing him good at last.

In the game against the Spartans he played as he had never played before. Twice in the first period he passed for assists that resulted in goals. Then, with twelve seconds to go before Line 2 had to get off the ice for the last time that first period, Biff came around the Spartans' net. He passed to Tod who was in a good position in front of the cage, and Tod smacked the puck in for his first goal of the season.

Coach Fillis shook Tod's hand as the boys skated off the ice for the intermission. "Good going, Tod," he said. "I knew you'd be coming along. You're a fast skater. Handling that puck takes time, and you're catching on now fine."

"Thanks, Coach," said Tod.

He assisted for another goal during the second period. The game was going strong in the White Knights' favor. When it ended, the score was 8-5.

"Nice game, Tod," someone said as they went off the ice.

Tod looked to see who had said that. It was Skip. He could hardly believe it.

"Thanks, Skip," he said. "Guess I just had a lucky day."

Riding home in Mr. Jones's car, Tod thought, *If I can just play all the other games as I did today, I could then feel that I could take that new hockey stick out of the closet. It would be wonderful to play with it. Just wonderful.*

They played the Trojans to a 3-3 tie on February 16. But Tod felt he didn't do well, that he still did not deserve the new hockey stick.

Manna Rink was crowded to the rafters the night of the Ice Show. Tod sat with Mom and Dad about halfway up and near the center of the row of seats. They had a perfect view of the show.

Below them a band started playing. A moment later, from both ends of the rink, the performers came skating in in two long lines. From the left were the boys, dressed in black tuxedos and stovepipe hats. From the right were the girls, wearing white blouses, white skirts, and white stovepipe hats.

And, trailing after the girls, then skating up between them and the boys, came the two smallest girls in the whole show!

"Mom!" cried Tod happily. "Look! It's Jane and Marylou!"

The crowd cheered and applauded. The noise almost crowded out the sound of the music.

At last the cheers and applause died away. Only the music was heard, mixed with the soft whispers of the skates. The skaters danced to the music, each boy finding a partner to dance with. Jane and Marylou danced by themselves. Tod watched unbelievingly. He had never dreamed that those two girls were that good.

He saw Ms. Hudson, too. And again he couldn't get over what he had once thought about her.

For an hour the show moved on with breathless beauty and excitement. Intermission followed. The crowd stretched their legs and many of them bought something to eat. After a while the show started up again. The spectators quieted down. The music played. The skaters reappeared on the ice.

The show was going along beautifully when suddenly a terrific blast seemed to rock the whole building.

People screamed. The skaters on the rink stopped dead.

Someone shouted, "Look!" Faces turned and fingers pointed toward the left end of the building. Thick, black smoke was belching through the doors. Seconds later, tongues of orange flame leaped out.

More people screamed. They rose from their seats and began hurrying to the exits.

A man shouted, "Don't panic! Please, don't panic!"

Tod realized it was Dad. He was standing up, his arms raised as he shouted. But few people paid any attention to him.

Down on the ice Tod saw the skaters heading for the exits, too. He couldn't see Jane and Marylou. Already a lot of the spectators had gotten on the ice. Many of them, while trying to hurry, had fallen.

"Tod! Mary!" cried Dad. "Go down there, find the girls, and take them out! I'm going to call the Fire Department!"

11

D AD VANISHED IN the crowd.

For a while fright gripped Tod. He took Mom's hand and felt her sweating palm against his. He looked at her and saw her eyes searching the rink.

"We must find Jane!" she cried.

They squeezed through the rows of seats to the aisle. People pushed, stumbled. Some fell. Whistles shrilled, and Tod saw several policemen trying to keep the crowd from getting panicky. They did not have much success.

Tod and Mom reached the aisle. They walked down the wooden steps to the cement walk that ran between the seats and the sideboards. They started for the gate that was down at the end of the rink. But the crowd held them back. It would be ages before they'd reach it and get on the ice.

Tod stared worriedly at his mother.

"Let's climb over the boards!" she said.

She lifted herself up on them, swung her legs over and jumped to the ice. Tod sprang over them and was instantly beside her.

"You're in good shape, Mom!" he grinned.

They held each other's hand as they tried to hurry across the ice. But hurrying was difficult, and Mom had trouble staying on her feet. She hung onto Tod's arm as tightly as she could.

They looked and looked for Jane. They came face to face with many of the performers but not Jane.

And what of Marylou? Perhaps the two girls were together. But where were they?

"Mom!" a voice shouted. "Mom! Tod!"

They turned. There was Jane, almost lost among the grown-ups who were trying to cross the ice. She skated toward them and swung her arms around Mom, almost knocking Mom down. She looked up. Tears filled her eyes.

"Marylou's back there!" cried Jane. "She fell on the ice! I think she's sprained her ankle!"

Mom's face turned white.

"Let's go after her," she said.

"Tod! Mrs. Baker!"

They looked around and saw Ms. Hudson skating toward them. Together they went after Marylou. They found her about ten feet away. She was on her feet, but unable to skate. She was crying.

"I can't move!" she sobbed. "I can't move!"

Tod's heart pounded. Marylou wasn't very big, but still she would be almost too heavy for him to carry. Then he thought of a way.

96

He got in front of her, turned around and crouched on his haunches.

"Climb on my back," he said. "I'll carry you piggyback."

She got on his back, and he started to carry her off the ice. This way she hardly felt heavy at all.

They reached the gate. Smoke poured thicker now from the end of the building. Flames were eating through the wood partition. It wouldn't be long before the fire reached the roof.

Tod choked back tears. He was thinking, *What if this beautiful building burned down? There would be no more skating. No more hockey.*

Where were those fire engines? Had Dad called them yet? What was delaying them?

Tod, Mom, the girls and Ms. Hudson just reached the exit when men in yellow slickers came rushing in, carrying water hoses. They were here!

Outside, a fireman wearing a Fire Chief's

helmet stopped shouting orders as he saw Tod staggering out of the building with Marylou on his back.

"Is she hurt?" he asked.

"Her ankle is sprained," said Mom.

"Let me take her," said the Fire Chief. "I'll have one of the men put her in the ambulance and take a look at her ankle. Don't worry. She'll be all right."

He took Marylou off Tod's back and started toward the white ambulance that was parked nearby. All at once a man and a boy came running forward.

"Chief!" the man shouted. "Chief Brown! Just a minute!"

Tod stared. It was Mr. Farmer and Joe. They ran up to the Fire Chief and Mr. Farmer took Marylou into his arms. They stood talking with Chief Brown for a moment, then the chief led them to the ambulance.

"Let's go to our car, Mother!" cried Jane. "I'm freezing!"

"Dear me!" Mom said. "I'd practically forgotten you have so little on! Do you want to come with us, Ms. Hudson?"

"No. I have my own car. Brrr! I'm freezing, too! Good night! I'll see you tomorrow, Tod!"

They walked hurriedly to their cars. Jane did the best she could with her skates on. Mom took a set of keys out of her purse and got in behind the wheel. Dad, she said, would come home with the fire truck. That might be in the wee hours of the morning.

As she drove out of the parking lot, Tod looked back at Manna Rink. Huge searchlights shone on the building. Smoke poured through the windows where the fire had started. Flames licked through the outside wall.

Tod turned away. He didn't want to look anymore. He closed his eyes and prayed that Manna Rink would still be there in the morning.

12

THEY DIDN'T GO to bed. Mom said she would stay up and read until Dad came home. She wouldn't be able to sleep, anyway.

Tod and Jane persuaded her to let them stay up, too. They changed into their pajamas and sat on the sofa together. They read books. Every once in a while Tod glanced at the clock on the television set.

They sat there almost an hour. Then Jane

began to yawn. She yawned several times. Finally, she said that she was going to bed. Mom took her.

"Good night, Tod," said Jane, yawning again.

"Good night, Jane," Tod said, and had to yawn, too.

Half an hour passed. It was eleven o'clock, and Dad wasn't home yet.

Tod reached the bottom of the page and realized he didn't remember a thing he had read. His mind was on Manna Rink. He was thinking of those frightened, screaming people. He was thinking of his dad. He was thinking of the flames licking at the walls like the hungry tongues of a thousand dragons.

Manna Rink is gone. It'll burn to the ground. There will be no more hockey games for us this year.

And what of my brand-new hockey stick? Oh, why did I make such a stupid promise? Why?

Twenty-five minutes after eleven. There was the sound of a motor outside. And voices.

"Dad's home!" cried Tod.

He dropped his book and rushed to the window. Mom went with him. They pushed the draperies aside and looked out. They saw the fire truck, its big headlights shooting huge beams through the darkness.

A moment later the truck drove off, and Tod saw Dad coming up the walk. Mom opened the front door for him. Her face was filled with anxiety, just as Tod's was.

Dad came in. He looked tired. He was still wearing a yellow slicker and a fireman's helmet. Mom closed the door and Dad stood in front of it. He looked from Mom to Tod. His face was as sober as could be.

"Why aren't you in bed?" he asked seriously.

"Dad!" Tod almost shouted. "How about Manna Rink?"

A smile flashed across Dad's tired face. "Oh,

one end got scorched. A partition was pretty badly destroyed. But that's all."

Tod's eyes widened. "You mean the roof didn't burn? You mean Manna Rink is still *there?*"

Dad put his arm around Tod's shoulder and gave him a firm hug. "Of course, it's still there. Matter of fact, I'm sure that hockey will keep going on as scheduled."

"Whoop-e-e-e-e-e!" shouted Tod.

"Sh!" Mom said. "You'll wake up Jane. Oh, I'm so glad that the fire didn't get any worse. What a shame that it happened tonight."

The ache in Tod's heart melted away. He felt so happy he wanted to wake up Jane anyway and tell her the good news. But Mom wouldn't let him. He could tell her in the morning, she said.

He went to bed and fell asleep almost instantly.

He talked with Ms. Hudson the next day.

She already had heard the good news about the rink. She said that she felt sure there would be no more Ice Show this season but hoped that there would be one next year.

"I called up Mrs. Farmer this morning," said Ms. Hudson. "Marylou's ankle is a little better."

That evening, after supper, someone knocked on the door. Mom answered it. It was Mr. and Mrs. Farmer.

"Please come in!" she said.

Marylou was with them. She limped when she walked, but on her face was a bright, happy smile.

"Just wanted to tell your son how thankful we are about the way he took care of Marylou," said Mr. Farmer. "Guess I was so scared something real bad had happened to her last night that I didn't even think about asking who had brought her out of the building. Later on it was Marylou, herself, who told me."

"We thought that was pretty quick thinking, Tod," said Mrs. Farmer happily. "And it took a lot of spunk, too. We are all very grateful to you."

Tod blushed. "Lucky she wasn't very heavy," he said.

They stayed a while longer and talked with Mom and Dad. Then they left.

About seven-thirty the phone rang. Tod didn't think it was for him, but he answered it.

"Tod?" a voice said.

"Yes, this is Tod."

"This is Mr. Haddock, Skip's father," said the voice. "I'm on the Father and Son Banquet Committee, Tod. The banquet will be held in honor of the boys who are playing hockey. The date is February twenty-eighth. The place, Packer Hotel. The time seven o'clock. Got all that?"

Tod swallowed. "Yes, sir."

"Fine. Don't forget. Tell your dad about it, and make sure you both come. You can pick up

106

your tickets Saturday at the rink. It's reasonable
—ten dollars will cover both of you. Good
night, Tod."

"Good night," said Tod.

He hung up. His neck was red as he rose and
went into the kitchen.

"Who was that?" Mom asked.

Tod shrugged. "It wasn't anything important," he said.

13

TOD TOOK a drink of water, then went to his bedroom. From the top shelf of the clothes closet he lifted off his large drawing tablet and carried it into the dining room. He got a pencil and tried to think of what to draw.

Everyone else was in the living room. Dad had his shoes off and was reading the newspaper. Mom was reading a women's magazine. Jane was in her little rocking chair "feeding" her doll from a bottle.

For a while Tod sat there with the blank paper in front of him. He couldn't think of what to draw because he was thinking of that telephone call from Mr. Haddock.

He didn't want to tell Dad about the Father and Son Banquet. Of course, Dad might consent to go. He might not want to hurt Tod's feelings.

But Dad didn't care for sports anymore. Not since he had injured his knee while skiing. And what did he know about hockey? Nothing.

A lot of those other fathers had played hockey. Most of them could skate. Some of them were coaches of the teams in the young boys' league. What would they think of Dad, who hadn't seen a hockey game yet this year?

Of course, Dad worked Saturday mornings. But there had been practices at Manna Rink three nights a week just before the league games had started. He would have attended one or two of them, at least, if he had felt any interest, wouldn't he?

Tod felt sweat on his palms and rubbed it off on his pants. Thinking about Dad and the Father and Son Banquet kept his mind from thinking about what to draw.

He went to the bookshelf in the living room and picked out a volume of the encyclopedia. Probably that would give him an idea.

He turned the pages and came to pictures of sailing ships. That's what he would draw. A ship sailing on the high seas. He started to copy it from the book.

After a while he forgot about the Father and Son Banquet.

That Saturday morning he walked into the dining room and stopped in his tracks. Someone was sitting there at the table he did not expect to see.

"Dad!" cried Tod. "You're not working this morning! Are you sick?"

"I'm perfectly fine." Dad smiled. "I told you I'd take off one of these Saturdays, didn't I?"

"Yes!" Tod was so thrilled he went over and gave Dad a hug.

He didn't say anything to Dad about the hockey game. But that was why Dad was home today. He had switched with another fireman just to attend the hockey game this morning.

Tod called Biff, and Biff said he and his mother would go with his, Biff's, father.

Dad drove. Jane and Mom went along, too. Tod was sick when he saw one end of Manna Rink so badly burned. But men had already begun repair work on it.

The game was with the Vikings. From the moment of the first face-off, the White Knights had possession of the puck most of the time. Joe Farmer tried twice to drive in the puck, but both times the Vikings' goalie made a save.

Tod sat nervously waiting for Line 2's turn

111

on the ice. He was thinking of Dad. How would he play today with Dad watching?

After he was on the ice for a few seconds he felt better. He intercepted the puck on a pass from a Vikings player and passed it to Biff. The pass was good, and Biff dribbled it across the Vikings' blue line.

A little while later Skip had the puck. He dribbled it down to the corner, came around behind the net and passed it to Snowball.

Two Vikings players charged in. Snowball passed the puck to Tod, who was in the right-hand circle in front of the cage. Tod picked up the pass. He dribbled a short way and then quickly snapped the puck to Skip, who was skating toward him from the other side.

Skip took the pass and slammed the puck into the net.

"Nice shot, Skip!" yelled Coach Fillis from the sideline. "Nice pass, Tod!"

White Knights hockey sticks thundered against the boards.

Later, the Vikings showed that they weren't there just for the exercise. They moved ahead of the White Knights. In the second period Tod made another assist as he passed to Jim Wright and Jim scored their goal. But as the game progressed the White Knights proved to be no match for the Vikings today. They lost the game 4 to 2.

It wasn't until they were in the locker room and began talking about next week's game that Tod realized there was only one game left to be played. One game left! And he had yet to play with his new hockey stick!

"Played a nice game, Tod," smiled Coach Fillis. "You got two points today. Assists count, too, you know."

Tod smiled. "Yes, I know."

He had done well. He was improving. But, somehow, he felt he wasn't doing well enough to deserve that hockey stick in the closet.

Perhaps it would remain there until next year.

113

"Did you get your tickets to the Father and Son Banquet?" asked Biff. "I got mine."

Tod's face reddened. "Not yet," he said.

From that second on the Father and Son Banquet lingered on his mind. He kept thinking about it in the car.

I don't want to ask Dad because I'm ashamed, he thought. *I'm ashamed that he doesn't like sports as the other fathers do.*

But it wasn't right not to ask Dad. Tod knew that. He thought and thought about it. And it was just before they reached home that Tod made up his mind.

"Dad," he said, his heart pounding, "there's going to be a Father and Son Banquet in honor of the hockey players. It'll cost ten dollars. Would you like to go? You don't have to if you don't want to."

Dad looked at him. He hesitated, as if he were trying to decide.

He won't want to go, Tod thought. *Just watch. He won't want to go.*

114

Then Dad said, "I think I'd like it very much, son. I'll be glad to go."

14

"HI, TOD! HI, Joe!"
"Hi, Ted!"

Tod stared up at his father, and then at Mr. Haddock, Skip's father.

"Do you know him, Dad?" Tod asked surprisedly.

"Of course. He and a lot of these fathers belong to the same club that I do."

116

Tod's jaw sagged. And he had thought all the time that his father was a stranger to these men!

Dad greeted other fathers, too. And they greeted him, shaking his hand as if they were really pleased to see him.

Boy! thought Tod. *And I almost made the mistake of not asking Dad to come!*

They found seats beside Mr. Farmer and Joe. Waiters and waitresses brought in the dinners, and everyone began to eat. There were ham and potatoes, all kinds of vegetables, and pie a la mode for dessert. Tod ate till he was stuffed.

Afterward there were speeches, including one by the coach of the university's hockey team.

It was a night Tod would long remember. He was really glad he had asked Dad to go. Both he and his dad had had a great time.

The last game was on March 2 at eleven o'clock. The White Knights tangled with the

Spartans. Dad worked until ten-thirty, then drove to the game with Mom and Jane. Tod went with Biff and Biff's father.

The Spartans had won only two games during the season, but they started playing as if they were champions. Center Cliff Towne socked in the first goal, then a Line 3 player for the Spartans smacked in the second.

Joe Farmer scored first for the White Knights, making the score 2-1. Then Line 2 came on the ice.

For a minute and a half the two lines played hard without either gaining any advantage over the other. Then Skip board-checked a Spartan player and was sent to the penalty box for one minute.

During that minute the Spartans tried desperately to raise their score. Three times Tim Collins made saves that drew loud applause from the White Knights' fans. And twice a White Knight wingman cut in, racing in

118

front of his own goal crease, to knock aside the puck that might have gone in for a score. That wingman was Tod Baker.

Tod didn't dribble the puck. He knew he had improved a lot at dribbling, but there were times when he would still hit the puck too hard. He didn't want to take those chances in this final game of the season.

So every time Tod got the puck he passed it to one of his teammates who was in the clear. And his passes were almost always perfect. The puck would glide across the ice just far enough in front of the receiver so that he would not have to slow down to pick it up on his stick.

Do I deserve my new hockey stick now? thought Tod. *I think I've improved a lot. But this is the last game. And the hockey stick is at home.*

With fifteen seconds to go before Skip's penalty time was up, Tod, Biff and Jim passed the puck among themselves down the ice deep into Spartan territory. The Spartans' defensemen charged in, tried to block the players and to steal the puck. The puck skittered up the ice. Tod spun around and raced after it. Just before it touched the blue line he hooked it with his stick, taking it away from a Spartan player.

Tod pulled the puck in front of him and then passed it to Biff, who was over near the boards. Biff caught it and passed it back to Tod as Tod raced for the net. Tod saw Jim skating up from his right side and passed the puck to him. Jim took it, dribbled it in front of the Spartans' net and snapped it.

Goal! And made while one of their own men was off the ice!

Then Skip came in. The White Knights were playing with their full force again.

Tod puffed as the buzzer sounded, and Line 2 got off the ice. He was tired, but he felt good. His passes were working smoothly. And he had scored a point by getting that assist. What a tough minute that was while Skip was resting in that penalty box!

Line 3 of each team scored a goal and the first period ended with the score tied, 3-all.

The locker room was noisy with talk as the boys filed in to rest. Most of them bought soft drinks to quench their thirst. They were happy, excited. The score was tied, but each team felt that theirs would be the winner.

Then Mr. Farmer, Mr. Haddock and some other fathers walked in. Behind them came Coach Fillis and — Tod stared with surprise — Dad.

They stopped in front of Tod.

"You're playing better hockey than you have all season, Tod," said the coach.

"Thanks, Coach. I've been trying."

"I've been talking with Coach Fillis about you," said Dad. "I told him about that brand-new hockey stick that sits in your clothes closet."

Coach Fillis shook his head unbelievingly. "Tod, there are very few boys who would wait

121

to use a new stick until they'd earned it. Takes a lot of gumption."

"We kind of think that you deserve that hockey stick now, Tod," said Dad.

Tears almost came to Tod's eyes, but he held them back.

"But—but my stick's home, Dad. It's too late."

Dad grinned. "I'll be right back," he said.

He was gone for a minute. When he returned he had the brand-new hockey stick with him.

"Had it in the car." He smiled. "Coach Fillis told me you were good enough to play with it last week. Or even before that. Here, let me take that old stick. You won't need it anymore."

When Line 2 skated onto the ice that second period, a brand-new hockey stick flashed brightly. Something about it seemed to do things for Tod Baker that the old one had never done. His face was radiant, his heart lighter. He seemed to skate faster than he had ever skated

before. He didn't dribble much, but he did a lot of passing.

Cries that he had never heard before now filled his ears almost every time he passed the puck.

"All right, Tod!" yelled Biff. "Nice pass!"

And when Tod made two beautiful assists to Skip in rapid succession that resulted in two more goals for the White Knights, Skip said:

"Beauties, Tod! Perfect passes!"

When the game ended the score was White Knights — 7; Spartans — 6. The White Knights were the league champions with five wins, two losses and two ties.

White Knights hockey sticks thundered against the boards. On the ice, White Knights players jumped and hugged each other. Up in the seats Tod saw Mom, Dad and Jane clapping and smiling with joy.

The teams poured into the locker rooms. Coach Fillis's face beamed with pride. He congratulated the boys. Then he paused in front of Tod.

"Guess our wingman can really play hockey, can't he, fellas? You know how many assists he had? Five!"

"Terrific!" cried Biff.

Joe Farmer shook his head. "Imagine keeping a brand-new hockey stick in a closet because he didn't think he deserved it," said Joe. "Man, that took nerve!"

"Nerve?" echoed Skip. "You mean guts!"

Tod looked at Skip. His eyes went big and proud. Coming from Skip, that was a wonderful compliment.

How many of these Matt Christopher sports classics have you read?

- ❏ Baseball Pals
- ❏ The Basket Counts
- ❏ Catch That Pass!
- ❏ Catcher with a Glass Arm
- ❏ Challenge at Second Base
- ❏ The Counterfeit Tackle
- ❏ The Diamond Champs
- ❏ Dirt Bike Racer
- ❏ Dirt Bike Runaway
- ❏ Face-Off
- ❏ Football Fugitive
- ❏ The Fox Steals Home
- ❏ The Great Quarterback Switch
- ❏ Hard Drive to Short
- ❏ The Hockey Machine
- ❏ Ice Magic
- ❏ Johnny Long Legs
- ❏ The Kid Who Only Hit Homers
- ❏ Little Lefty
- ❏ Long Shot for Paul
- ❏ Long Stretch at First Base
- ❏ Look Who's Playing First Base
- ❏ Miracle at the Plate
- ❏ No Arm in Left Field
- ❏ Red-Hot Hightops
- ❏ Run, Billy, Run
- ❏ Shortstop from Tokyo
- ❏ Soccer Halfback
- ❏ The Submarine Pitch
- ❏ Tackle Without a Team
- ❏ Tight End
- ❏ Too Hot to Handle
- ❏ Touchdown for Tommy
- ❏ Tough to Tackle
- ❏ Wingman on Ice
- ❏ The Year Mom Won the Pennant

All available in paperback from Little, Brown and Company